Beneath the Bridge

by **HAZEL HUTCHINS**

art **RUTH OHI**

ANNICK PRESS
TORONTO ♥ NEW YORK ♥ VANCOUVER

Beneath the bridge
water flows.
Where it's headed
no one knows.
Traveling merrily along–
my small boat.

Beneath the bridge
water flows.
Where it's headed
no one knows.
Frogs goggle, rushes grow.
Insects hover to and fro.
Traveling merrily along—
my small boat.

Beneath the bridge
water flows.
Where it's headed
no one knows.
Frogs goggle, rushes grow.
Insects hover to and fro.
Who is swimming, who is resting?
Who is flying, fishing, nesting?
Not so merrily along—
my small boat.

Beneath the bridge
water flows.
Where it's headed
no one knows.
Frogs goggle, rushes grow.
Insects hover to and fro.
Who is swimming, who is resting?
Who is flying, fishing, nesting?
Buildings snuggle by the shore–
a house, a church, a grocery store.
Look, oh look! A red canoe
has saved my boat. They like it too!
Traveling merrily along–
my small boat.

Beneath the bridge
water flows.
Where it's headed
no one knows.
Frogs goggle, rushes grow.
Insects hover to and fro.
Who is swimming, who is resting?
Who is flying, fishing, nesting?
Buildings all along the shores—
houses, churches, grocery stores.
Where is everybody going?
Like the water, they keep flowing.

POPCORN

People from the red canoe
have passed my boat to someone new!
Traveling merrily along—
my small boat.

Beneath the bridge
water flows.
Where it's headed
no one knows.
Frogs goggle, rushes grow.
Insects hover to and fro.
Who is swimming, who is resting?
Who is flying, fishing, nesting?
Buildings crowd along the shores—
houses, churches, grocery stores.
Where is everybody going?
Like the water, they keep flowing.
Cars and trucks on ribboned roads.
Diesel trains with heavy loads.

The motor launch comes in to shore
and hands my boat along once more!
**Traveling merrily along–
my small boat.**

Beneath the bridge
water flows.
Where it's headed
no one knows.
Frogs goggle, rushes grow.
Insects hover to and fro.
Who is swimming, who is resting?
Who is flying, fishing, nesting?
Buildings march the crowded shores—
houses, churches, grocery stores.
Where is everybody going?
Like the water, they keep flowing.
Cars and trucks on ribboned roads.
Diesel trains with heavy loads.
Giant ships, giant cranes,
giant dock spouts loading grain.

The *River Queen*, can it be true?
They're talking to that huge ship's crew!
Traveling merrily along—
my small boat.

Beneath the bridge
water flows.
Where it's headed
no one knows.
Someday I'll follow, just to see,
but for now it sails for me.
Traveling merrily along—
my small boat.

For the times, sweetest of all,
when we travel side by side.
—H.H.

For Dad
—R.O.

Annick Press Ltd.
All rights reserved. No part of this work covered by the copyrights hereon may
be reproduced or used in any form or by any means – graphic, electronic, or
mechanical – without the prior written permission of the publisher.

We acknowledge the support of the Canada Council for the Arts, the
Ontario Arts Council, the Government of Ontario through the Ontario
Book Publishers Tax Credit program and the Ontario Book Initiative, and
the Government of Canada through the Book Publishing Industry
Development Program (BPIDP) for our publishing activities.

Visit us at:
www.annickpress.com

Cataloging in Publication

Hutchins, H. J. (Hazel J.)
        Beneath the bridge / Hazel Hutchins, Ruth Ohi.

ISBN 1-55037-859-7 (bound).–ISBN 1-55037-858-9 (pbk.)

        I. Ohi, Ruth II. Title.

PS8565.U826B45 2004   jC813'.54   C2004-901089-1

Distributed in Canada by: Published in the U.S.A. by Annick Press (U.S.) Ltd.
Firefly Books Ltd.   Distributed in the U.S.A. by:
66 Leek Crescent   Firefly Books (U.S.) Inc.
Richmond Hill, ON   P.O. Box 1338
L4B 1H1   Ellicott Station
                                   Buffalo, NY 14205

Printed in China.